Pippin Takes a Bath

For Ashley Samantha Lee — K.V.J.

For Adrian, Meredith, Julian, Patrick, Allie,
Brandon and Megan — B.L.

Text © 1999 K.V. Johansen
Illustrations © 1999 Bernice Lum

Kids Can Press acknowledges the financial support of the Ontario Arts Council, the Canada Council for the
Arts and the Government of Canada, through the BPIDP, for our publishing activity.

Published in Canada by
Kids Can Press Ltd.
29 Birch Avenue
Toronto, ON M4V 1E2

Published in the U.S. by
Kids Can Press Ltd.
2250 Military Road
Tonawanda, NY 14150

www.kidscanpress.com

The artwork in this book was rendered in watercolor and marker.
The text is set in Smile.

Edited by Debbie Rogosin
Designed by Marie Bartholomew
Printed and bound in Hong Kong, China, by Book Art Inc., Toronto

The hardcover edition of this book is smyth sewn casebound.
The paperback edition of this book is limp sewn with a drawn-on cover.

CM 99 0 9 8 7 6 5 4 3 2 1
CM PA 02 0 9 8 7 6 5 4 3 2 1

National Library of Canada Cataloguing in Publication Data

Johansen, K. V. (Krista V.), 1968–
Pippin takes a bath

(Pippin and Mabel)
ISBN 1-55074-627-8 (bound).   ISBN 1-55337-420-7 (pbk.)

I. Lum, Bernice II. Title. III. Series: Johansen, K. V. (Krista V.), 1968– . Pippin and Mabel.

PS8569.O2676P56 1999   jC813'.54   C99-930241-8
PZ7.J617ZPi 1999

Kids Can Press is a Corus™ Entertainment company

Pippin Takes a Bath

Story by K.V. Johansen

Illustrations by Bernice Lum

Kids Can Press

Pippin was a
yellow dog
with great
big ears and a
curly, black tail.

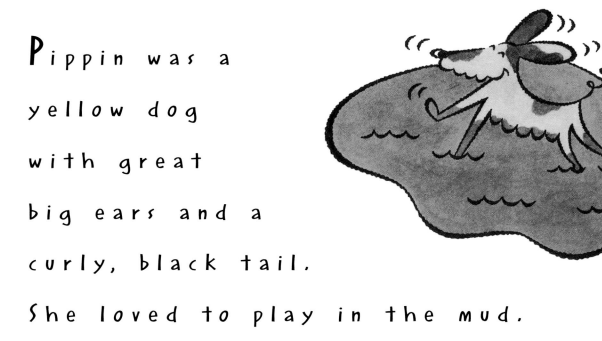

She loved to play in the mud.

One day Pippin found a big
mud puddle. She splashed in that
puddle, splish! splash! splosh! until
she was muddy from her ears to
her tail.

Then she went home.

"Oh Pippin," said Mabel. "You're too muddy. You can't come into the house like that."

Mabel put away her paintbrushes.

She set a big metal tub in the yard and filled it with water.

Pippin hated baths! She hid in the rosebushes.

Mabel pulled Pippin out, picked her up and put her in the tub.

Zoom! went Pippin. She raced out of the yard and through the field. She jumped into the ditch and peeked out through the cattails.

"Come back here!" shouted Mabel. She ran through the field until she came to the ditch.

"Aha!" said Mabel, and she tried to grab Pippin. But her foot slipped and Mabel plopped into the mud.

"Ribbid!" said a frog.

"Woof!" said Pippin.

Mabel went back to the house and took a bath. Pippin had to stay outside.

The next day Mabel said, "Right, Pippin. Today you will have a bath."

She filled the big metal tub with water. Pippin hid in the toolshed. Mabel hauled Pippin out, picked her up and put her in the tub.

Then she picked up the shampoo.

Zoom! went Pippin.

Bloop! went the shampoo.

Pippin dashed out of the yard,

through the field and over the ditch.

She crossed the brook on a log and

hid in some prickly blackberry bushes.

"Come back here!" Mabel shouted. "You need a bath!"

Mabel ran out of the yard and through the field. She jumped over the ditch and stepped onto the log.

"Aha!" said Mabel. And she tripped. Right into the cold water she fell!

"Quack!" said a duck.

"Woof?" said Pippin. She licked Mabel's face.

Mabel went back to the house and sat in a hot bath and drank tea. Pippin had to stay outside all alone.

The day after
that Mabel said,
"Pippin, today
it's your turn
to have a bath."
She marched

_Phew!

Pippin into the house and
upstairs to the bathroom. Pippin
darted away and hid in a closet.
Mabel dragged Pippin out, carried
her to the tub and turned on
the water.

Zoom! went Pippin.
Splash! went Mabel.
Pippin dashed down the
stairs and out the door.
She galloped out of the yard,
through the field, over the ditch,
across the log and into the woods.

Mabel leapt out of the tub. She ran out of the house, through the field and over the ditch. She hurried across the log into the woods.

Pippin tried to hide in a fox's hole, but it was too small.

Then she tried to climb a tree, but she couldn't.

"Pippin, come back!" called Mabel.

Then Pippin saw a pile of rocks. It looked like a good place to hide. But something was sleeping there in the sun. It was black and white. It wasn't a dog, and it wasn't a cat.

"Woof?" said Pippin.

The skunk woke up.

It stamped its feet

and waved its tail.

"Yip!" Pippin yelped.

What a smell! What a

horrible smell!

It stung her eyes

and her nose and her

throat. Pippin ran

and ran and ran,

but she couldn't run

away from that smell.

Pippin rolled in the brook, but that didn't help. She rolled in the grass, but that didn't help either. She rolled in the muddy

ditch, but she couldn't get rid of that smell.

Pippin ran to Mabel and jumped up on her and whined.

"Oh Pippin!" said Mabel.

Mabel took Pippin home. She put on her oldest clothes and set the big metal tub in the yard.

Pippin's ears drooped and she put her tail between her legs. But she got into the tub all by herself.

First Mabel gave Pippin a bath
with tomato juice.

Then Mabel gave her a bath with vinegar. Pippin whimpered. It smelled almost as bad as the skunk.

"This is what happens to dogs who get sprayed by skunks," said Mabel, and she gave Pippin another bath, this time with smelly shampoo.

Finally Mabel dried her with a big green towel.

But Pippin still smelled like a skunk, so she had to stay outside.

The next day Pippin took another bath. And the day after that, another. And at last Mabel let her come into the house again.

Then it rained. The mud puddle got bigger and bigger and bigger. Pippin put one paw in it. The mud oozed between her toes. It was sticky and smelled like rain and old leaves.

Pippin jumped in with all four paws. She splashed in that puddle, splish! splash! splosh! until she was muddy from her great big ears to her curly, black tail.

Then she went home.

When Mabel saw Pippin, she sighed, and then she laughed.

"Oh Pippin," said Mabel.